Eva and Sadie
and the Best Classroom
EVER!

By Jeff Cohen • Illustrated by Elanna Allen

Eva and Sadie
and the Best Classroom EVER!

HARPER

An Imprint of HarperCollinsPublishers

For Grammy, Grandpa, Lela, Nana, and Papa.
You make everything better, too.
—J.C.

For Sarah
—E.A.

Library of Congress Cataloging-in-Publication Data
Cohen, Jeff (Jeffrey Brandt), date. author.
 Eva and Sadie and the best classroom ever! / by Jeff Cohen ; illustrated by Elanna Allen. — First edition.
  pages cm
 Summary: Sadie, who is about to start second grade, decides it is up to her to make sure her little sister, Eva, is ready for kindergarten.
 ISBN 978-0-06-224938-8 (hardcover)
 [1. First day of school—Fiction. 2. Kindergarten—Fiction. 3. Sisters—Fiction.] I. Allen, Elanna, illustrator. II. Title. III. Title: Best classroom ever!
 PZ7.C6626415Eum 2015   2014034159
 [E]—dc23   CIP
                                                                                        AC

The artist used pencil, watercolor, and a touch of Adobe Photoshop to create the illustrations for this book.
Typography by Jeanne L. Hogle
15 16 17 18 19 SCP 10 9 8 7 6 5 4 3 2 1

First Edition

I'm Sadie, and this is *my* little sister, Eva.

I'm about to start second grade. I can tell time and I can even read books by *myself*. I know a lot, but beginning second grade is still a pretty big deal.

Eva is about to start kindergarten. That's a big deal, too. Kindergarten is *completely* different from preschool.

First, there are no naps in kindergarten.
This could be a problem for Eva.

My dad says if Eva doesn't get a good nap she gets super grumpy.

So, on weekends, when she's supposed
to be napping, I keep Eva awake.

After all, it's *my job* to get Eva ready for kindergarten.

Also, lunch is completely different.

In preschool, Eva brought her lunch from home every day.

But in kindergarten, she has a choice—bring your own or buy it there. Just like a big kid.

That makes Eva really nervous. It's a big decision.

I tell her the biggest difference between kindergarten and preschool is . . . there's just so much to learn!

She'll have to learn about math and writing and reading and that kind of stuff.

Of course, I already know how to do those things. But Eva doesn't. And I don't want her to feel nervous on her first day. That would be sad.

This means one thing. I've got a lot of work to do.

At our house, we made our very own classroom. It has everything I need to get Eva ready.

Sometimes, I let Eva lead the class.

But most of the time, I'm the teacher. There's no time to waste!

Here are a few things I do to get my sister ready:

I take attendance.

It's important to be
on time in kindergarten.

I use flash cards so Eva can
learn important words before
the first day of school.

I teach her all of the songs
I learned in kindergarten.

LUNCh

We pretend to wait in line
at the cafeteria.

And I quiz her to make sure she
remembers what she's learned.
Eva's been working super hard.

"Sadie, what's a
minus sign look like?"

"I only know how to write my name."

"Aagh!"

Oh, and we also go outside for playground tests.

When Dad comes home, Eva doesn't even look up to say hi.
That's when I know things aren't working out the way I planned.
"Eva," Dad says. "Can you at least say hello?"

"Not now, Daddy.
I'm trying to focus."

"Sadie's helping me get ready for kindergarten," she says.

"I have math sheets to do and I don't even know what math is.

"The monkey bars make my hands hurt. And I'm worried about the cafeteria, too."

Uh-oh. This is bad, bad, bad.

I didn't mean for
Eva to get so upset.

"Sadie," Mom says.
"She's only five."

"But she's got to be ready for school," I say. "And if I don't help her, who will?"

"You've done a great job," Dad says. "But Eva doesn't have to know everything on the first day."

"And don't forget, you didn't have a big sister to help
you get ready for kindergarten and you did just fine."

When the first day of school comes, Eva is still nervous about lunch, so she decides to take matters into her own hands. While everyone else is still getting dressed, she goes downstairs and gets whatever she can find.

Guess what she makes? Peanut butter and chocolate syrup on an onion bagel. It doesn't sound like a good lunch to me, but it makes her feel a lot better.

Mom and Dad are surprised when they come downstairs.

But I'm proud of her.

"Nice work, Eva!" I tell her.

On the way to school, Eva tells *me* she has butterflies but I remind her I'll be nearby.

After the morning assembly, Eva and I go to our separate classrooms. And that's when *I* get nervous.

Will she remember everything I taught her?

Will she be able to write her name?

Will she be able to do the monkey bars?

Is she really ready for kindergarten?

When school is over, I run right to Eva's classroom to make sure she's okay.

And guess what?

I poke *my* head in, and I see Eva—she isn't doing math, she isn't practicing her vocabulary words, and she isn't taking a test.

Guess what she *is* doing?

She's playing with two new friends. And she's happy.

I guess Eva is ready for kindergarten after all.